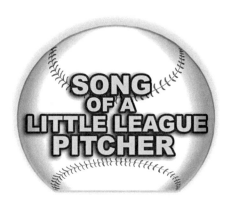

SONG OF A LITTLE LEAGUE PITCHER

WRITTEN BY ERIN O' CONNOR
ILLUSTRATED BY MIKE GOLDSTEIN

Dedication...Song of a Little League Pitcher...

This book is dedicated to the Little Leaguers, past and present, who "light up" my life:
Luca, my grandson and present day "player extraordinaire".
Devin and Donovan, my sons, loyal to El Segundo Little League throughout their boyhoods.
My husband Brooks, a Venice, California Little Leaguer of the 1950's.

Summary:
This book is not a simple story. It is a poem depicting the inward journey of a nine years old pitcher and his personal relationships with the game, his catcher, his coach, teammates and fans.

A percentage of the proceeds from the sales of Song of a Little League Pitcher will be donated to California Little League.

I invite my readers to visit my website The Eyes Of Erin...www.theeyesoferin.com to find out about all my books and the charities affiliated with each.

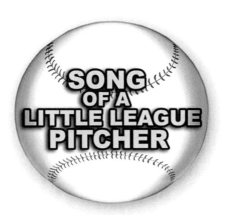

SONG OF A LITTLE LEAGUE PITCHER

Author
Erin O'Connor

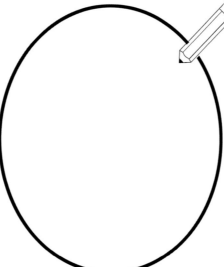

Reader
This book belongs to:

- - - - - - - - - -

Illustrator
Mike Goldstein

A Message to My Readers

Baseball is a wonderful sport. It was invented in America 150 years ago and is now played all over the world. I have realized, however, that my readers might not know anything about the game and how it is played. Because of this, I worry that you may have trouble truly understanding "Song of a Little League Pitcher".

Therefore, before you read this poem/story, I suggest you take the time to read "Baseball Handbook" which appears as a book within a book at the end of "Song". I have explained baseball as simply as I can. My illustrator, Mike, has drawn pictures to help you, the reader, grasp the meaning of the different statements. He has made this section like a coloring book so that you can have fun as you learn.

Your Friend,

Erin O'Connor

I woke up in the dark of night.
My heart was pounding hard with fright.
The fear of loss was creeping in.
I thought, "My team has got to win!"

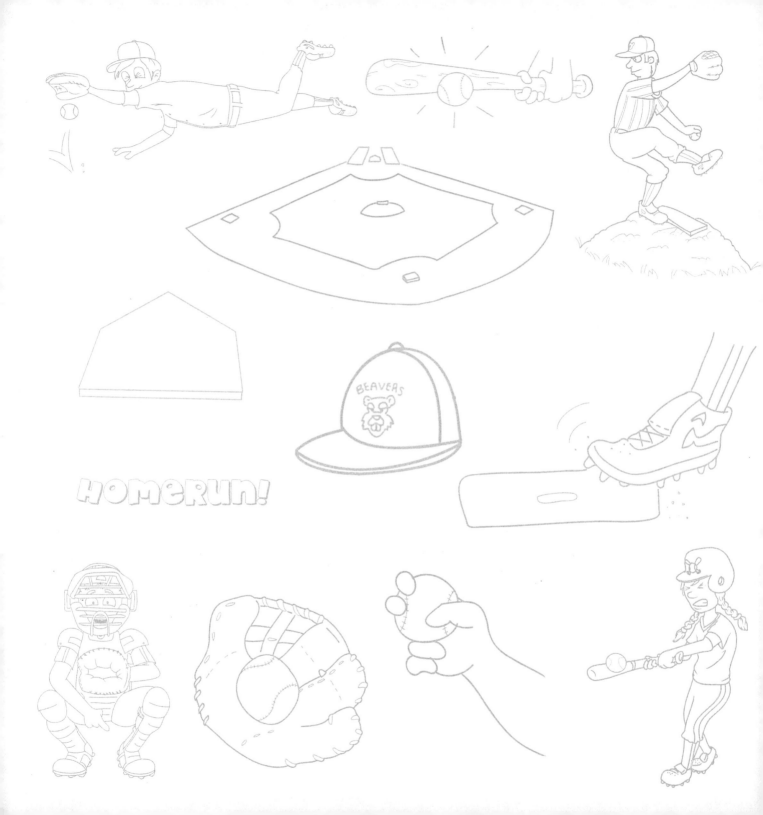

HOMERUN!

BEAVERS

So what if it was 4 A.M.
Got out of bed right there and then.
I showered long to calm my nerves
And thought about my pitching curves.

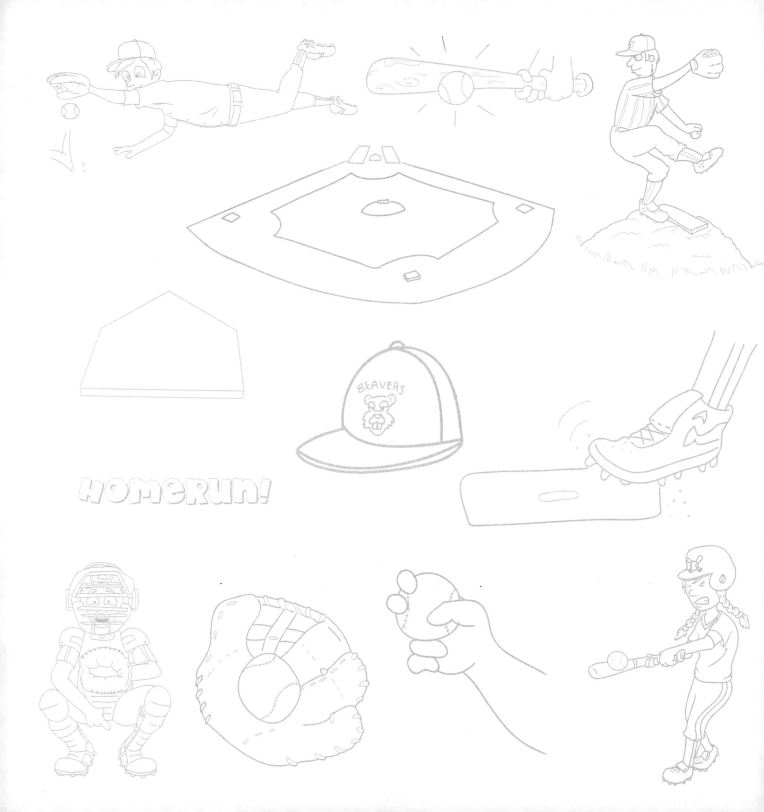

HOMERUN!

BEAVERS

Quietly I dressed and ate
While thinking of some pitching "Greats".
Though only nine, I knew the minds
Of champion pitchers from all times.

HOMERUN!

I left a note for Mom and Dad.
I asked them, "Please, please don't be mad!"
And, even though it still was night
I didn't need to pitch in light.

I wanted to be best that day
So I could pitch one "all the way".
The Bears were hot, but I do know
The pitcher shapes a game with throws.

And if my throws were hard and fast,
And if I could be cool and last,
Then we would win the baseball game
And make the crowd go quite insane.

HOMERUN!

I stopped to pick up Jeff, my friend.
I snuck up to his house, and then
I told him I felt so up-tight
And he agreed to help me fight.

HOMERUN!

BEAVERS

For four long hours, from five 'til nine,
We worked and worked so I'd do "fine".
I knew if I could just control
I'd be a pitcher to my soul.

Before the game was going to start,
I "chugged" some orange juice for "heart".

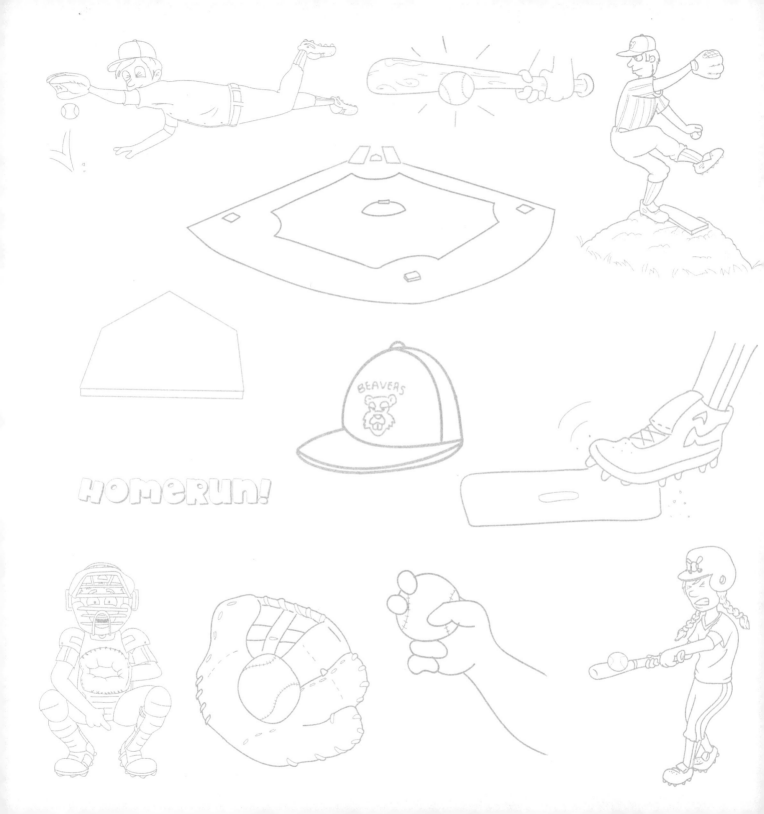

Then, with a winning attitude,
Stepped out to pitch fast, hard, and smooth.

The first two innings were a breeze.
The Bears were cold and hard to please.
Six struck out, six in a row,
They couldn't hit my awesome throws.

The coach was thrilled. He patted my back
And said, "You're great kid...that's a fact!"
His words were magic to my heart.
It made me proud to play my part.

HOMERUN!

The bottom of the fourth was rough.
The Bears came on real fast and tough.
Three to zip...the Bears were mad!
They gave the Beavers all they had.

I gave up one, a man on first,
Then Richie doubled in a burst.

But I was cool...I seized control
And struck out three men in a row.

HOMERUN!

The crowd grew wild...they cheered me on
But I remained an even calm.
I hit a double in the fifth
And Joe ran home on my fine hit.

The final inning looked a breeze.
Five runs ahead kept me at ease.
I had just one thing on my mind...
I wanted this game to be mine.

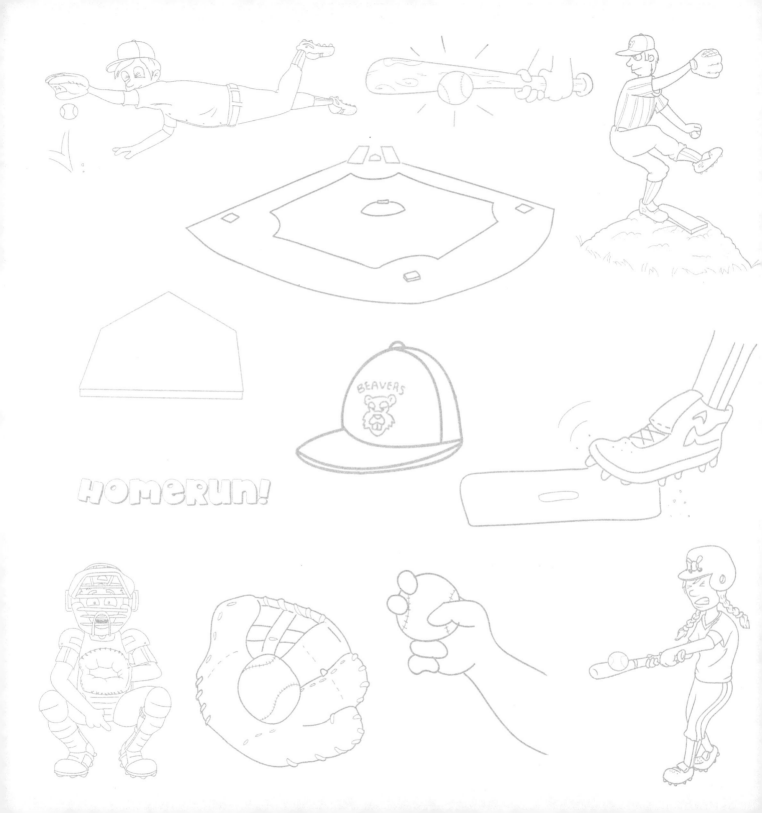

HOMERUN!

With batter one, I had no prob.
But batter two was one hard job.
I felt his strength on his first swing...
A triple...Wow, that ball had wings!

HOMERUN!

But four hours practice from before
Kept my attention on my chore.

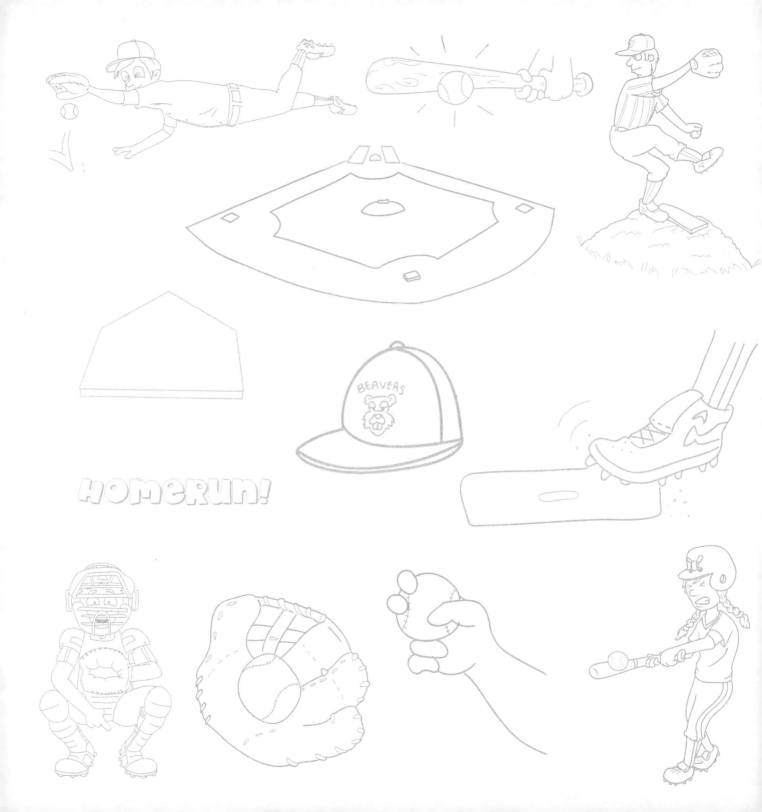

HOMERUN!

Controlling my fantastic power
We shut them out that very hour.

The fans were thrilled with such a win.
They ran onto the field and then
A ton of arms tossed me around.
Then, suddenly, I left the ground.

HOMERUN!

"What a game," I thought that night,
The game I played so clean and tight.
Then deep within my "pitcher soul"
I felt the pride...I'd pitched my goal.

Baseball Handbook

HOMERUN!

Baseball was invented in America. For 60 years, from 1838-1898 baseball evolved and changed until the rules we now use were perfected. It is a favorite pastime in the United States and all over the world.

HOMERUN!

Baseball is played on a baseball field that looks like this....

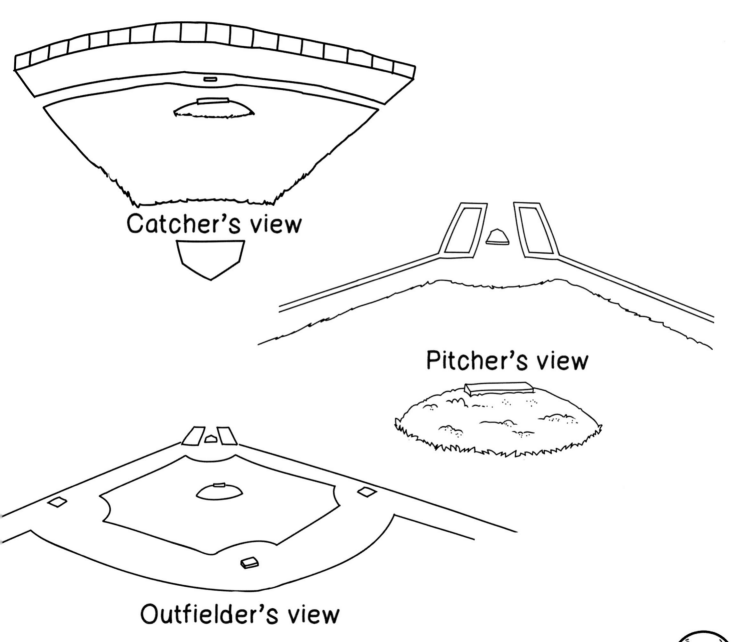

Catcher's view

Pitcher's view

Outfielder's view

25

HOMERUN!

Baseball is a team sport. There are nine players on a team. Two teams play each other.

Baseball players wear uniforms and use baseball equipment.

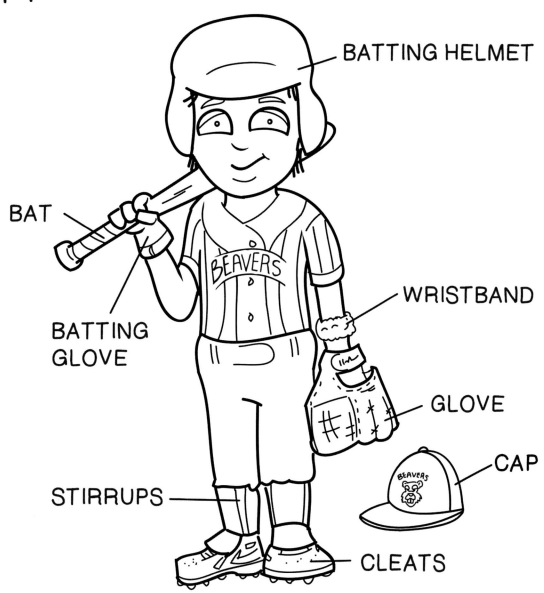

BATTING HELMET

BAT

BATTING GLOVE

WRISTBAND

GLOVE

CAP

STIRRUPS

CLEATS

BEAVERS

HOMERUN!

Every team has an adult called the coach. The coach teaches his players the skills of baseball, the rules of baseball and how to play with great sportsmanship.

Every player learns to hit the baseball with his/her bat, catch the baseball in his/her glove, throw the baseball and run the bases.

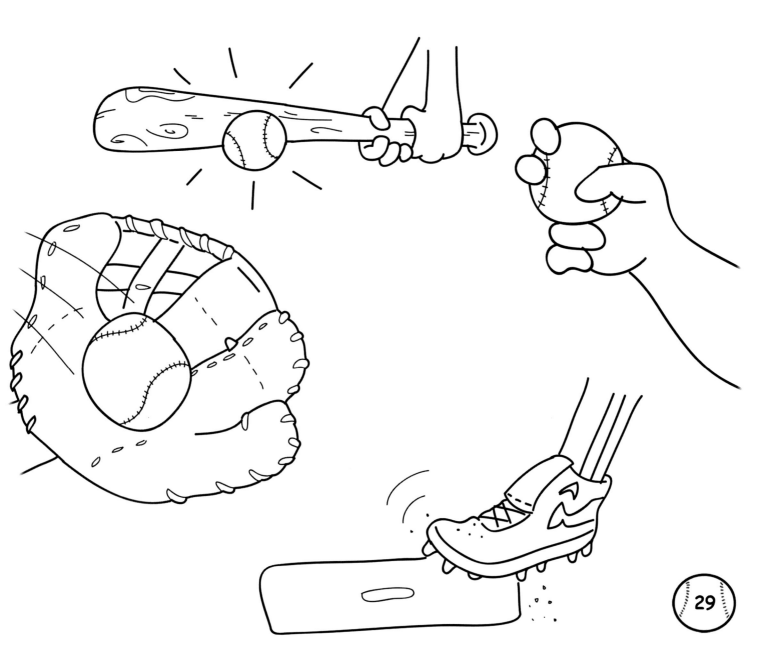

Baseball is divided into innings. During an inning, the batting team tries to score runs while the fielding team tries to prevent runs.

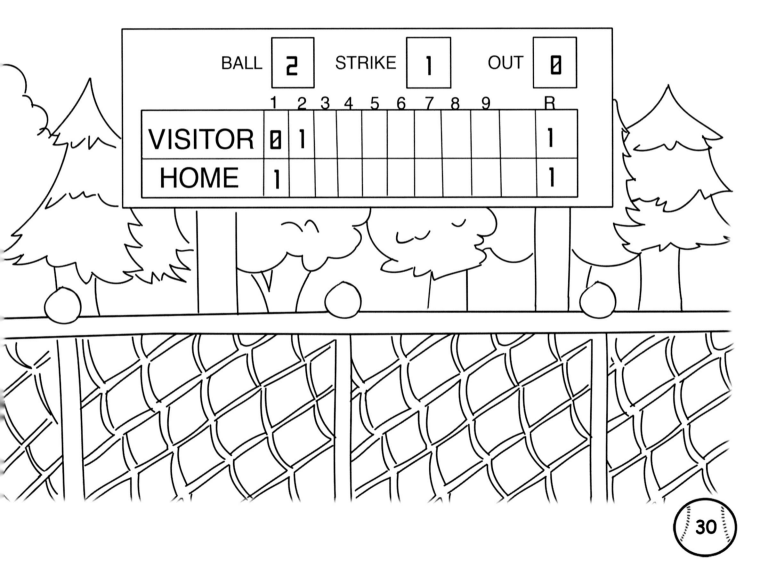

	BALL	2	STRIKE	1	OUT	0

	1	2	3	4	5	6	7	8	9	R
VISITOR	0	1								1
HOME	1									1

HOMERUN!

When a team is up to bat, each player sits on a bench in an area called the dugout. Each player waits his/her turn to bat.

When a team is on the field, each player plays his/her position. These positions are: pitcher, catcher, 1st baseman, 2nd baseman, 3rd baseman, shortstop, left fielder, center fielder, and right fielder.

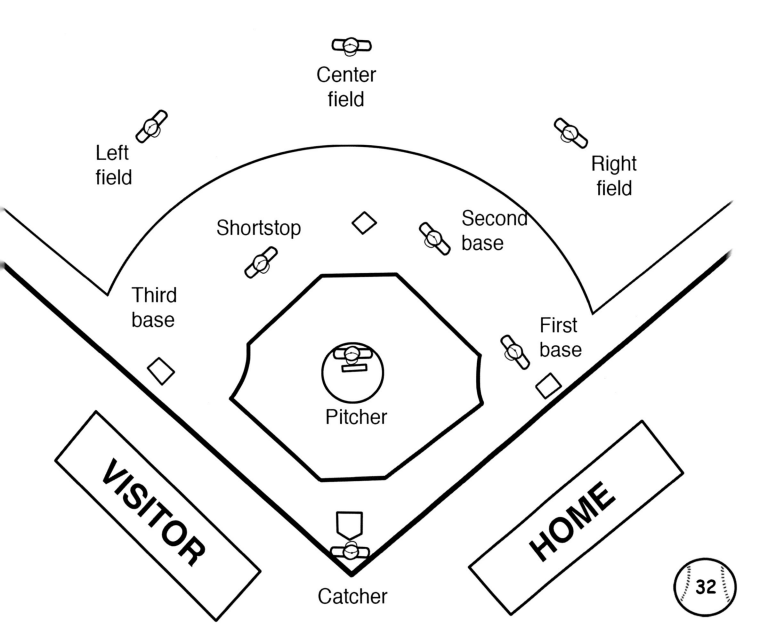

Center field

Left field

Right field

Shortstop

Second base

Third base

First base

Pitcher

VISITOR

HOME

Catcher

32

HOMERUN!

The pitcher is a very important player. He/she throws different types of pitches (fast balls, curve balls, sliders and others) to one batter at a time. His/her goal is to confuse the batters with different pitches and keep all batters off base.

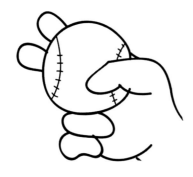

Fastball

Curveball

Slider

The catcher's job is to catch all the pitches.
The pitcher and the catcher are a team within a team.
The catcher gives the pitcher secret hand signals to
decide what type of pitch should be thrown.

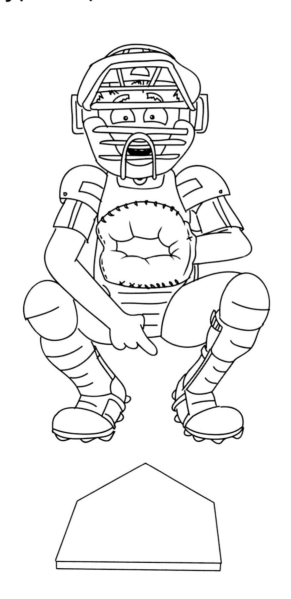

HOMERUN!

In addition to the pitcher and the catcher, the 1st baseman, 2nd baseman, third baseman and shortstop protect the "infield". The left, right and center fielders protect the "outfield".

HOMERUN!

BEAVERS

Baseball can be a frustrating game. When a batter hits the ball (which is not easy), a few things can happen:

The batter hits a home run...(the ball goes into the stands and the batter runs all the way home)

HOMERUN!

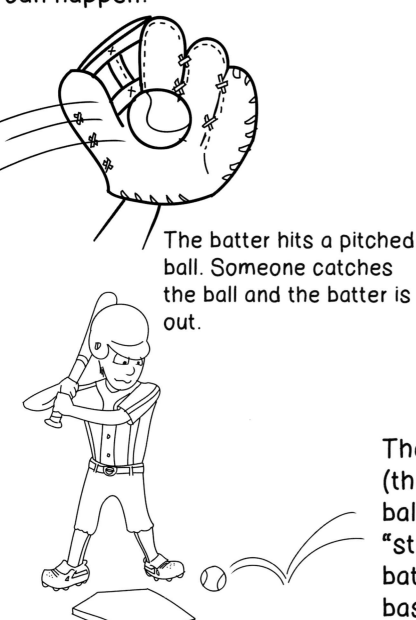

The batter hits a pitched ball. Someone catches the ball and the batter is out.

The batter walks... (the pitcher throws 4 balls which miss the "strike zone" and the batter goes to 1st base)

The umpire stands behind the catcher and decides if a throw is a ball or a strike. The umpire calls a player safe or out.

HOMERUN!

Each time a batter runs all the bases and makes it back to home base, he/she scores a run.

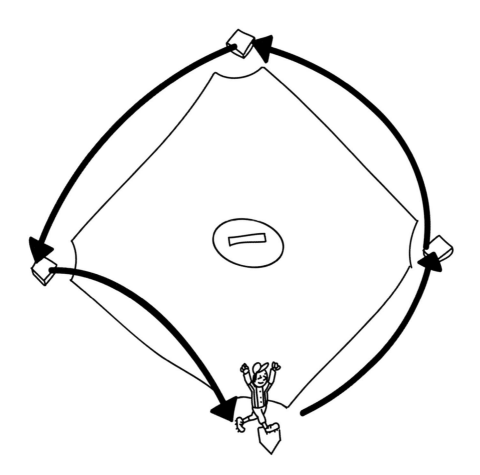

Playing baseball takes a lot of energy. Eating and drinking healthy foods is very important.

HOMERUN!

For all the players, especially for the pitcher, baseball is all about focus, calm and strategy. It is an amazing feeling to pitch a great game.

For the batter, it always feels great to hit the ball.

HOMERUN!

BEAVERS

The fans who watch baseball are terrific. They cheer for their teams. This positive energy gives power to the players and makes the game fun!

The End.

Do you want to know more about the author?
Do you want to know more about the illustrator?
Need lesson plans? If so, visit www.theeyesoferin.com

HOMERUN!

BEAVERS

43923072R00052

Made in the USA
San Bernardino, CA
01 January 2017